FOR GOD SO LOVED.

BY: GLORIA ADWOA AMOANIMAA KONADU

It was 2018, and Justine Was

home by herself alone. she usually is,

she works as a nurse and work all sorts

of odd hours. Justine, a young lady of

28 years old is someone who didn't

believe in God, an atheist. she felt

everything she has accomplished in life

she has done by herself and her own

right thinking has brought her to her

job, her financial security, and basically

everything she has attained in life. She

knew a little bit about the Bible and

when others approached her regarding her beliefs, she would always say, "judge not lest Ye be judged."

One day while going through Facebook she got a message from an old schoolmate. his name was Kevin. They knew each other when she was young in primary school.

At first, she ignored the message because she didn't want to be bothered by a man. But a few weeks went by and she saw the message again it said I am not sure if you are

the same person whom I knew as a

child, but I think you are, and I would

like for you to contact me.

she recognized his face he had

not changed much. She sent a reply to

his text on Facebook chat texting,

"How are you, Kevin? Yes, it's

me."

Kevin promptly replied, back to her. He

was able to contact her and once they

spoke with each other, they talked for

hours. She felt a comfort with him that she had not felt with any other man.

It was around Christmas time and Kevin was about to go to his work Christmas party and felt that he would like to go with Justine. She, all of a sudden, change character and let him know that she's not interested in dating right now. He wasn't surprised by her answer.

He let her know of his intentions that he always fancied her when they were children, and he is a Christian he will not like to impose his beliefs on her but rather he would like for her to learn for herself and understand God's purpose for her.

She hanged up the phone and forgot about him. Justin worked in the ER of a hospital and one night while working a night shift, somebody tapped her on her shoulder.

The person was none other but Kevin, he had a broken ankle. he was on crutches. At first, she smiled and then said hi to him, and then moved away from him. As if she was busy doing something; he slipped her a note and left. when she got home that morning from the night shift, she was so tired she took her shower and went straight to bed.

When she awoke, she had seen a piece of paper on the floor of her bedroom and it was the note that Kevin had slipped in her nursing uniform. It said, "For God so love the world, that he sent his only begotten son and that whosoever believes in him shall not perish but have everlasting life". Then she crumpled up the paper and threw it in a dustbin. She turned away and didn't see that the note didn't land in the dustbin but rather bounced off the tip of the dustbin and fell on the floor.

She didn't want to have anything to do with Jesus. Because where was

Jesus when her boyfriend made her get rid of her first child, where was Jesus he was nowhere to be found she felt she had attained everything on her own merit without the help of any God and so therefore why was this love that Kevin was talking about. She felt very angry at Kevin for him to Impose his beliefs on her.

She thought who is this Kevin?, we knew each other as children yes but now I'm a grown woman I put myself through school I have my own

job I have my own house and I had no

help from any man.

She went about her day for rest

of the day. A few weeks passed and

when she was doing her cleaning, she

found the paper on the floor next to

the dustbin. She opened it up and

read the note again. Then she had a

feeling to go online and find out about

that quotation.

She went to google and typed in those words "For God so Loved the World". It brought out from the search engine; {John 3:16}. She read through the whole verse and started to think about the things that she's been through. How could people believe in such drivel. Who is this GOD and who is his son? Where were they, when her boyfriend made her eat rice filled with rat droppings. Where were they when he let her go bankrupt twice and is still resettling from paying debt that

is not hers.

Who is THIS GOD, and his son

and where is this their LOVE. She got

so upset and frustrated that she

knocked over the lamp that was over

the laptop. As she was upset, a song

by a singer by the name of Adwoa

Konadu came on titled "Let Go".

It went like this "How long can

we keep inside, the things that keep on

stressing us. That's infested our hearts

and destroying our lives, can we let

go? Someone has let the past

experiences fester within the mind and

the heart, can we let go? How long will

we keep inside the things that has

been festering within our hearts and

our minds. Someone has let the past

experiences fester within the heart

and the mind. Can we let go? It's time

that we open our heart and let God be

filled within us, and change our lives,

can we accept him? How long can we

keep inside the things keep on

stressing us. That's infested our hearts

and our minds, can we let go?"

She started to cry as she listened

to the song. The singer started off the

song by saying that "Avail yourselves

and Let the Holy Spirit work within

you. Let it take any pain or hurt that

has caused you to be in a state of mind

that is causing your progress in some

areas of your life".

When the song finished, she picked up the phone and called Kevin. The phone rang about 3 times and then he picked up. He was concerned because of the state of how Justine was through hearing her crying at the other end of the phone. She let him know that she feels that she is having a mental breakdown and didn't have anyone to talk to and so she just picked up the phone to call him. He asked her to keep calm and to breath in and out. He talked calmly with her

to calm her down so, as to not arise

her anxiety.

Kevin asked her what triggered

her sudden burst of anxiety and has

she been through anything traumatic

to bring on the outburst? She narrated

hearing the song and the words within

the song after getting upset and

reading "For God so Loved the world".

Kevin then asked her "What did

she think of the verse?" She said "that

coupled with the song on the t.v. is

what triggered her upset and anxiety."

She said "I started to recollect all the

many times in my life that I was in

trauma and was in pain. I didn't feel

the love of this GOD and his son. Also,

why would he send his son? What did

the son do for me?"

Kevin then started to let her

know that "The Son", Jesus, came to

die for our sins and cleanse us of our

sins. If and when we confess our sins to him. He is the way, the truth, and the light. No one comes to the father except through his son, Jesus.

She then started to become interested in what Kevin was saying. She stopped crying and Kevin made sure she was alright before setting up a date for them to discuss more on who Jesus, the son of GOD is.

Kevin set up a date at his place. He prepared a meal for her and when she arrived, he ease her composure by asking her what songs she liked and they played it on YouTube for her to listen before they started to read The Bible.

He first started with The Promises that God has for us his Children. It says in Psalms 46:10 "Be still, and Know that I am with you". Meaning even though your world may be turned upside down, know that he knows and is with you. All the trials that you've been through Like the

singer Adwoa Konadu sings in her

song; "He knows it all": "When times

get hard, and you feel afraid, Look to

the Lord, for he knows your fate. Look

to Christ, He is for you, Your trials, your

pain, He knows it all."

As they got to meet each week,

they got closer with each other and

like the love Justine has now

developed for Christ, Jesus grows so

has her love for Kevin. Because "FOR

GOD SO LOVED", so has that love

changed Justine through Kevin and her

availing herself and letting the POWER

of the HOLY SPIRIT work within her

and allowing GOD to reach her before

she was too far gone in her own anger,

anxiety and lack of acceptance of men

in her life.

THE END ☐.

About the Author

I am a Medical Secretary who used to live in Canada but has now moved to Ghana. I love writing, singing and my family and friends as well as the life that GOD has blessed me with.